Champagne

Christine Péquignet

To my daughter.

Watching her grow up inspires my own growth.

Table of Contents

Champagne 1

The sunseeker 3

Aloha 9

The stone cutter 13

Reflective ocean 15

Spectrum of dreams 19

Window seat 23

Polite triviality 27

Disenfranchised grief 29

In my footsteps today 37

A blanket of clouds 39

Our own boat 43

Feeding the fish 45

A bag of rice 47

The shape of what will be 51

ACKNOWLEDGMENTS

This book is the byproduct and the testimony of a journey I took inside myself. Thank you to everyone who helped me on this journey. Thank you to those who encouraged me to write and publish this book. You saw an ability that I did not think I had. Thank you to those who inspired me, you might not even know you did. Maybe you will recognize your contribution in this book.

I was lucky to benefit from the professional help of Sam Barlow and Ben Masters who each with their own trade, made this book possible. You both gave me tools I will use for the rest of my life.

https://sambarlowtherapy.co.uk/

https://www.benmasterscopy.co.uk/copywriting/

Champagne

I am a bottle, or I was. For years I crushed grapes and hid them inside. I lay there on the rack and bubbled inside.

Recent times have shaken the bottle. And now the cork has popped, and the bubbling liquid cannot be contained. It is flowing out, it is foaming and expanding, it is exploding, and it is messy.

Quick. Bring the glasses. Fill them up and serve them to your friends. The grape is barely recognizable, and it stings the tongue. Some will really like it; others won't. Each glass is a story, an emotional release.

I am now a book, and each page is a story. I serve them here to my friends and hope they like them. Some won't.

CHAMPAGNE

The sunseeker

I live in Britain, and to adapt to life in this country, by politeness or necessity, I have perfected the art of discussing the weather. It came naturally to me as my life had always been paced by the ebb and flow of atmospheric pressure.

When I was 8, after the most exciting and sunny summer spent with my grandmother, she passed away. At the ripe age of 97, it shouldn't have come as a surprise, but for someone my age, it was inexplicable. The news came on a grim rainy Monday of October. I did not understand death. We never saw my grandmother again and slowly reality set in; she was gone for ever. Trying to make sense of it, I blamed the weather. The summer sun had brought joy, tasty fruits, and laughter. The cold grey rainy days could only bring misery. I got validated when the next summer was rainy and not nearly as lively. I had discovered the weather's power to affect not only people's mood but also their fate.

When my parents went through a rough patch, my dad changed job and we moved from Normandy to Provence. It could have been the better job, the bigger house, my dad's newfound sense of purpose, but I decided the weather had brightened our household mood. Yet a few years later, I moved to Paris to study geology. When a sad breakup sent me into a prolonged melancholy, I resolved to move south again. Upon graduation, I landed a post in Marseille and welcomed the opportunity to move to a balmier climate.

Life was good again. The job was fascinating, with adventurous field trips to the Sahara which exposed me to more heat and sun than I had ever known. Scorching temperatures turned out to induce mostly serious headaches and severe sunburn. Sun-drenched climates did not protect me from life's difficulties. My colleagues were friendly, and we worked passionately for long hours towards a common goal. But for all the wonderful geological treasures we discovered, the project still failed to find what it intended. The large contract that was supposed to follow remained as elusive and finally after 3 years, our beloved company closed its doors. Unemployed, without friends, I found my life was heading towards drought.

Determined to bounce back, I sent my CV everywhere, for jobs in the Arctic, to a wintering position in Antarctica. I was edgy during an interview with a Norwegian company. The 8-year-old me kept telling the 28-year-old me that Norwegian weather would only bring gloom. The rational scientist I had become couldn't give credit to her silly childhood belief. But childhood beliefs can be very stubborn, and persistent. When the choices narrowed down to a 2-year contract in Gabon or a permanent position in northern Sweden, I called it intuition rather than irrational childhood belief and packed my shorts and sandals. Gabon was hot and exotic. The job was rewarding, if maybe slightly unethical. But a hefty salary has a way of taming the inner voice, and it becomes easy to overlook one's principles when your bank account fills a lot quicker than it empties. Two years turned into four and I settled in this easy life. I found a loving partner and soon we welcomed ten adorable little fingers and toes. Our daughter was perfect. Life could not get any better. Is it the mountain of nappies, or the sleep deprivation? Is it the hours staring lovingly at her, or the immense joy when she ran to my arms after a day in childcare. The unrestrained joy of a toddler, and how your hug can stop her cries. All of this changed me. Children wrap your heart with embracing arms and reach deep into your soul. Their innocence penetrates levels of wisdom and self-awareness you did not know you had.

One day, watching my daughter jumping in muddy puddles, I couldn't push away something that had been nagging me for a while. Scruples. How could I keep contributing to an industry that was destroying her planet? What would I tell my daughter when she would confront me about the perils of our climate? I could lie to myself and justify staying in this job, but would I be able to lie to her? Staying in this life became intolerable. 8-year-old me awoke again and directed me towards the gentle sway of the trade winds, the pleasant temperature of the tropics.

For a while life gifted us with a perfect climate and matching professional opportunities.

But the path to life is paved with chance and choices. My husband's parents needed help on the other side of the planet. Luckily or unluckily for us, the funding for our academic positions was also drying out and relocation was looming. With a heavy heart but a clean conscience, uncertain of our decision, we moved to Britain. There is little point in wondering if we made the right or wrong choice, it only matters what we made of it.

Three months after our arrival, on a sunny summer day, my daughter decimated my flower bed to make a fantastic bouquet to bring to her grandmother. Bright red dahlias are the last thing she saw when she closed her eyes for the last time. As it had been for me, losing her grandmother was the first tragedy our daughter had experienced. Her pain rained down her cheeks and on her favourite summer dress. As I wrapped my arms around her to try to ease her pain, I felt the sun, not the one that warms the skin but the one that warms the heart.

CHAMPAGNE

Aloha

Most of us don't remember playing that early game of sorting shapes in a box through their associated holes. It is an important skill that some animals have also mastered.

We may think we fit in the place where we belong, the place where we come from. For some, defining where you belong or where you come from is a difficult concept. If you have moved around or if you are multiracial or multicultural, it is particularly hard. But nevertheless, if we grew up in one environment, this is all we know and we may not question fitting in.

Travelling and meeting strangers expand your options, resets your certitudes, answering as many questions as it asks. Getting immersed in where you don't fit helps define where you do. If you are lucky like me, you might one day discover a hole that fits your shape better.

For me, this place is Hawaii. I see you sneer. Who wouldn't like the warm water, the palm trees, the beaches, and the luxuriant mountains. The Rainbow State, with its laidback Aloha spirit. A place where if you walked around with an iron board under your arm, people would mistake it for a surfboard. To anyone who lives there, you will know that Hawaii is also poor infrastructure, heavy traffic, sky-high cost of living, and its subsequent homeless problem.

To me, it was love at first sight, and smell, sound, taste, and touch. Hawaii appealed to all my senses. The sand between my toes, a butter mochi in my mouth, the fragrance of frangipani and mango, and slack-key music, how could I not feel at home? And then there is the camouflage effect. A place where no one asks me where I am from. My mixed-up accent, my skin tone, my indescribable appearance that does not fit in boxes. I am part of a visible majority in Hawaii. There is even a name for people like me. Hapa – the word refers to people of mixed ethnic heritage, and it is not derogatory. If anything, it is highly regarded. You carry in your blood customs from spread out lands that make Hawaii such a rich culture.

Today, I live far away on another island, and I miss Hawaii dearly. Particularly on rainy winter days. A French woman in post-Brexit Britain, not the greatest fit. But Hawaii helped me define who I am, and I can take that everywhere I go. I see a lot of people who think they don't fit in. Like fingerprints or snowflakes, we are all different. Fitting in is not about a place, or similar people: it is knowing who you are and what you bring to the world.

CHAMPAGNE

The stone cutter

There was a man who felt different and lived alone in a cave. He lived surrounded by rocks and knew all about sedimentary processes. When the villagers needed stones to build their houses, they would come to him. He would tell them where and how to get stones. But slowly he found it easier to just carve them himself. He would cut stones and leave them in a pile. He knew people needed stones and he wanted to contribute to building their village. Sometimes he was so busy cutting stones that he wouldn't see any villagers for days. He would deliver at night and felt like an anonymous benefactor. But losing touch with the people he served meant losing touch with their needs. He kept delivering stones of the same calibre and the piles remained unused because the villagers preferred bricks that were smaller and easier to handle. So, he cut the stone smaller and smaller. Soon he reached the very supporting rock of his cave. He kept cutting and one day his cave collapsed. His cave, his shelter was now a pile of stones of all sizes.

With no shelter and a pile of stones, he resolved to build a house for himself outside the village. He appreciated the grading of the stones and how big stones built strong foundations, but small ones allow for artistic details.

When his house was completed, it was beautiful. He offered the leftover stones to the villagers, delivering the many sizes according to their needs. Soon the village grew and reached his house, and he became a villager.

Reflective ocean

I am an oceanographer. Every day I aim to better understand the ocean to be able to predict its changes. I assess the skills of predictive models of the ocean and where the limits are in our understanding. I spent years dissecting the mechanisms of ocean waves. Waves are as fascinating to study as they are beautiful to watch. Beautiful and terrifying in many ways.

Recently I heard someone compare thoughts to waves, saying that "thoughts are no more separate from the mind than waves are separate from the ocean."

That got me thinking. At first, I dismissed it and thought it was not so. Waves follow rules and equations. But the more I tried to disprove the statement the more it made sense.

Waves need a force to generate them. Sometimes we don't see the origin because it comes from a remote place far away from where we are today. Sometimes we are in the middle of the storm. Waves build up and propagate and change some of their characteristics, and the longest ones reach deeper and further.

Waves don't just add up linearly: they can carry each other and generate other waves, or they can cancel one another.

They can squeeze in tiny gaps and come out bigger on the other side. They can change direction and align with the bathymetry that carries them.

Waves can destroy and waves can sustain. They can be enjoyed and can be feared. Waves are powerful and can be harnessed. But even the strongest wave will pass. You can take a photo, measure it, record it, but ultimately, the wave will dissipate.

Waves change as they experience different conditions and environments. When ocean waves enter an estuary or a bay, they are no longer deep ocean waves and become shorter and bigger; they can even resonate in a receptive harbour.

Waves can bounce and reflect, and they rarely stay unchanged for it. The backwash is not always predictable.

Two opposing waves can result in a stationary oscillation, a wave going nowhere.

You can try to understand them, to dissect them in their components. But their stochastic characteristics, their fleeting chaotic nature makes waves impossible to forecast with complete accuracy. Ask any expert in rogue waves, they will agree.

Yes, indeed, thoughts might be like waves. Enjoy them when they come and, if you don't, remember they will pass. Share them, bounce them; they won't feel as heavy when others carry them with you.

CHAMPAGNE

Spectrum of dreams

Dream job, dream house, dream partner. Why do we call dreams our aspirations, our goals, and ideals? The house I go to in the middle of my sleep is rarely the one I would want to build. Aspirations are a construct of the future. Dreams are a projection of the present. On the continuum of time, they probably meet somewhere but only partially intersect. Dreams might be the desires we do not see, the hopes we are not able to carry.

I once killed a friend in a dream. We were climbing an unrealistically high mountain of snow. The shape was like Rio's Sugarloaf but maybe 50 metres high. We were at the summit and this mountain was like an island we couldn't climb off. Following my middle-of-the-night instinct, I decided that if I swung the mountain back and forth, I would reach the climbing rope that was attached to the cliff that was nearby and we could get off. My trusty friend let me do it. Incredibly, my plan worked. The mountain was not firmly grounded and started to oscillate back and forth. I leaned towards the cliff. I had to time it right. When I thought I was as close as possible, I could jump and grab the rope. As I leapt in the air with my hand extended towards the rope, my instinct was to push myself to reach further. Two feet flat on the side of the mountain, I jerkily strengthened my legs, and got the momentum I needed to reach the rope. The mountain, at the apex of the oscillation and at a lull of its velocity, suddenly accelerated away from me and the cliff. The push had been enough to unbalance the snow mountain. As I felt the pressure of my feet on the mountain ease, I realized what was happening. I yelled to warn the people below before the mountain crashed down onto the snow-covered plain on which it stood. This avalanche of snow buried the plain under a layer much deeper than the amount of snow available could cover. Luckily, my warning was enough to send people to safety. All were safe, all but one: my friend. In the fall, she got crushed and suffocated under the snow.

When I walked around to inspect the situation and see if anyone needed help, everyone pointed their finger at me. "She is the one who killed her friend," they said.

Overcome by shame and guilt, I woke up.

None of this were my aspirations. I do not want to kill my friend, no more than I wanted to cover everyone with snow. I did, however, want to get off this snow mountain I was stranded on with my friend. There was no food, no warmth, nothing at the top of this mountain. We couldn't stay.

Someone had to do something. We had let the mountain get so high that smoothly sliding down its sides was not an option anymore. We would have crashed. I am covering everyone with my escape, and I carry the weight of the casualty. My village guilts and shames me for trying to save us, to save me.

The mountain is me. I am pushing against the person I have become, somebody I do not like and barely know, someone that only vaguely resembles the person I wished to become.

On the spectrum of dreams, where my aspirations, yearnings, and needs intersect, this is where I find myself.

CHAMPAGNE

Window seat

Thank you, Wright brothers, for aviation. You have opened the way to long-distance travel to the masses. In a world where time is money, it has even enabled fast and cheap short-distance flights that could easily be covered on the ground. But in taking away the slow passing of the scenery you have robbed us of the joy of travel boredom and the imagination that comes with it.

I am reflecting on this sitting on a train, slowly making my way across three countries to reach my destination. I will fly back, but I decided to take my time to get there. There is probably a strong symbol in my decision.

The monotony of endless fields has induced a semi- awake state that is prone to daydreaming and conversation with myself. I am reminiscing about my student days backpacking in cities we are now travelling through, and laughing to myself at how young and naive I was back then. It is pleasant to be plunged back in a time when life was easy. Light as a feather inside and out, it is a pleasure just to remember this time and I smile. A lady three metres away is watching me. My smile seems contagious.

This is the last train now, and the crowd is thinning. Time has passed in my daydreaming and memories too. I am now reflecting on more recent and serious events. Matching my mood, the landscape outside also seems more austere. The towns look older and more decrepit. Maybe it is just me: my obligations are tinting my glasses as I am remembering I am not backpacking but I am on a mission.

This is the last station before my stop. The train is nearly empty now. The lady is still here and still looking at me. As I realise that this travel companion is the only person I can see from my seat, she smiles at me. I smile back and suddenly she gets up, grabs her bag, and comes to sit next to me. In a panic I try to remember the phrases I had learnt to address the locals, and before I can remember any words, she starts:

- "Hi, it's only us now. Funny how we departed from the same city and are going to the same destination. "
- "Sorry, I hadn't noticed you."
- "I noticed you with your red coat. In a crowd of black and grey garments, I admired your red coat."

This comment makes me smile and brings me back to a less serious mood.

- "I guess I needed to be colourful for this trip. What a coincidence that we are taking the same trip and end up in the same carriage."
- "I can't claim responsibility for this. Someone else booked the tickets for me."

I do not reply, but I am sure my face betrayed my silence. I looked outside; she looked down. Neither of us wants to be the first one to reveal our goal. I am not sure why; on the return voyage my objective will be obvious, and I will have to tell everyone. But for now, I am not ready. Not ready to arrive. And the destination is quickly approaching. The trip was long enough, and I have been preparing for this day for months, years really. But can one ever really prepare themselves for what is about to descend on me?

After a succinct introduction from me, she tells me she is a psychologist. She apologizes for staring at me, but she was fascinated by my facial expressions. She had observed my inability to hide my emotions as I reminisced about my past brought up by the passing landscape. She had tried to guess the underlying feelings and was making up stories in her head to imagine what I was recalling. I blush, as if she could actually read my mind.

The train stops and we silently make our way to the front of the station. She seems as solemn and thoughtful as I am. I spot a man with a sign with my name... just above another name. I looked at her. She is staring at the man too.

She glances back at me, and in her eyes, I read my story. The years of trying to get pregnant, the repeated miscarriages. The excruciating pain, the impossible grieving for someone who never was. The snowball effect on my life. The loneliness and sense of failure, the guilt, the shame, and, finally the acceptance and, the decision to go another route. Another long and difficult route, but that ended with a phone call. The voice telling me they had a baby for me, a little girl that needed a home. The rest of the conversation is a blur. How deaf our ears become when our eyes are obscured by tears.

She nods at me, and we get in the car and drive to the start of our new life. Soon I will be too busy for that much pondering; there will be bottles and nappies, and, hopefully, naps.

Polite triviality

It is loud; everyone is talking and laughing. You smile shyly and try to engage.

Every conversation reminds you that you don't belong here. You have matching clothes and lifestyle, but you stand out like a sore thumb.

You feel eyes on you; you hear them wonder who you are and what you are doing here. But these eyes and voices are the ones you imagine, to tell yourself people had noticed you. You have learnt to blend in so well that you worry you are now camouflaged. You look around for the one person that looks like how you feel, and you go talk to them. You find yourself voicing platitudes and you dislike yourself for being capable of such polite triviality which you despise so much. You know exactly how these make the other feel. It makes them feel exactly like you feel, exactly how you don't want them to feel. If you are lucky, there will be one person who will look at you and catch your eye. They will smile at you with a smile that says more than a conversation. A smile that says, I see you, and you are not alone.

In your mind you try to balance time. How long do I have to stay to be polite, to make illusion and to actually force myself to immerse in a crowd in the hope that physical closeness will somehow permeate into my feelings? You remember the time when it wasn't like this. It is so long ago, or maybe just feels like it. You can't find a way back to that time. So eventually you retreat. You will match your environment with how you feel inside. You will plunge yourself into darkness and silence because it is easier to feel blind and deaf, to make your senses agree with your feelings. You might try to fill the emptiness with a bottle or with a tub of ice cream. This never works. The key to emptiness is to pour it out. To let it come and let it go. To cry or shout it out. To write it off or paint it down. To jog it off or sail it away. You don't fill emptiness, you dissolve it, by exploding it, smashing it against the world. Tomorrow the sun will rise, and the day might be easier. You will try again and hope your load gets lighter.

Disenfranchised grief

In my building there is Mr. B. on the first floor, the kindest old man I have ever met. Some say he lost his wife and his house in a fire a long time ago, and his son in a car crash a couple of years ago. On the 2nd floor there are Mr. and Mrs. L.; they don't have children, but have an annoying poodle, who I am sure has godparents, a savings account, and his own bedroom. Crammed in a small 2-bedroom on the 3rd floor are the C. family. They have 4 well-behaved, but loud boys. At least they are polite; they always say good morning when they run you over screaming down the stairs. The single guy on the 4th floor used to be so athletic. I am not sure what happened to him. He disappeared for a while and now he walks a lot. He removed the roof racks on his car, the ones that were always carrying surfboards, a kayak, or skis. The 5th floor family is the perfect textbook family. It is a surprise they even live here; they should have a house with a white picket fence. Mrs. T. is straight out of an American movie from the 50s. She brings baked goods to neighbours when someone is ill or just moved in or has a significant life event. Mr. T. works 9 to 5 and comes home to put his son on his shoulder and tickle his daughter. And then at the top there is me. If I judge myself the way I describe the neighbours, I should say: the single lady at the top is a busy person. She does a lot of volunteer work. She is well educated and has a massive bookshelf that you can see through the windows. Clearly, her career is her priority. The last few years, she has been putting on weight, and looks increasingly unhealthy. She should go for walks with the gentleman from the 4th floor.

The occupants of my building, with all their stereotypes, cover a good portion of the immense range of human loss. The pain of loss has no scale and can't be measured or compared. There are many flavours, many colours of loss.

Behind the cookies and the pampered poodle, behind closed doors, under the surface lie broken hearts.

On the first floor, Mr. B. has accepted and processed the pain of his loss. He has learnt to live on his own. He has found peace in the memory of his loved ones. He enjoys the freedom that a small apartment gives and focuses on others. Selflessness has become his guilty pleasure.

Mr. and Mrs. L. would have loved to have a child, or three, as she imagined when she was a schoolgirl.

She even had names ready. Instead, they had dogs, and gave all their love to the 4-legged friends. But dogs rarely survive their owner. It always comes too early, and every time, it reopens a wound. People will think it is just a dog and that they can get another one and they will. But after each dog, they feel increasingly disconnected from the people around them.

The 4 boys from the 3rd floor are a blessing. Having children was easy for Mr. and Mrs. C. He just had to look at Mrs. C. and she got pregnant. The kids are healthy and fill up her life, but she cried when Mrs. T. brought cookies to announce she was having a girl. He feels the pressure to provide for 4 growing boys, but he would not want his wife to work and not be able to look after the kids. She wanted to be a nurse, and has almost become one, given that one of the boys always seems to be sick or with a broken limb.

The 4th floor resident has seen his life shrink year after year. He used to have it all: the house, the white picket fence, a trophy wife, and a healthy son. He now has only the photos to attest to it. He didn't want a second child. His life had changed too much after just one, so he dragged his feet, avoiding making the decision to try for another child. His wife waited patiently for him to be ready, until it was too late and that broke her inside. Blinded by his indecision, he missed the turn, the subtle fork in the road, where she went one way, and he went the other. And from there it is all too familiar. By the time they realised how far they had drifted, they had irreparably hurt each other. She left with their boy. He threw his loneliness into sports. Until a wave that was too big, badly timed; a nasty wipe out followed. When the lifeguards got to him, he had been deprived of oxygen for a smidge too long; the neurological consequences are not visible, but he will never surf or ski again.

The 5th floor perfect family has a third child. She lives in an expensive institution that offers a lifestyle more suited to her limitations. No amount of baking will fill this void.

Unlike my 4th floor neighbour, my life has not shrunk. It has rather expanded, as the size of my bookshelf or my waistline testify. But lately it seems to spiral towards a funnel. As I am edging towards the silent alarm of my biological clock, I can't even lie to myself about how I feel. To lie I would have to know how I feel and tell myself the opposite. I don't even understand what I am about to lose. I know the alternatives: there is adoption or fostering. Getting a pet or focusing on my nephews.

How do you grieve the loss of something or someone that never was? How do you mourn a bond or longing you didn't even think you had? What photo do you put on the wall of someone that was never born? What memory do you have of an egg that never got fertilised? How do you acknowledge the end of the possibility? It's the end of a story that never started. The end of hope that you secretly had but never admitted, not even to yourself, because you always doubted the outcome. It is ripping the inside of your organs. That part of you which you never feel until it aches. You now understand why love is associated with a vital organ, because when love is in pain this is where it hurts. This love for a person that never existed, only in your dreams. It should be easy to forget something that is not real. But maybe dreams are real. They are the projections of real feelings that are buried so deep you cannot see them. A window on our inside world. A path to understanding who we are and what we want.

Reproduction issues start before birth. It is emotional, it is physical, it is hormonal, it started when I didn't get a Y chromosome. It started when the task of reproduction landed heavily on the female of our species. This responsibility has to be weighed against your choices, your life, your destiny. A weight that absence and loss can render heavier.

You are taught how to protect against pregnancy, but nothing prepares you for the life that you will never deliver. Not every woman will become a mother, no matter how much she wants it. Not all pregnancy ends in a baby. Statistics are clear. Advice on grieving is like advice on becoming an Olympic athlete. What matters are the hours, days, months, the time that passes slowly, the effort, the pain, and the litres of salty fluid, sweat, or tears. Talking about the lives that won't be or won't even be considered is not going to erode the pain, but this will erase some of the shame and guilt that comes with thinking you did something wrong, that you failed, that you are abnormal, incapable. Thinking about reproduction, it is easy to think that if there is an all-powerful creator, they may have indeed been male. In his immense wisdom, he realised the heavy toll inflicted on the female body. Preparing every month for potential conception and the work of carrying and delivering a life was probably best stopped in advanced age. Conversely, the male's role of Great Sower could easily last until death. This biological difference probably explains why most men's needs and desires don't change much over time, but women's go 180° around middle age. Thank you for the considerate touch of sending women symptoms to announce the decline of their reproductive role and possibility. We could have so easily failed to notice the end! I want to mention it did not have to be so: there are other possible biological models. Personally, I find the task-sharing style of the seahorse very poetic. But I am digressing.

I like my building, this microcosm of human experiences. I particularly enjoy the caring cookies from the 5th floor. I should tell her I got a new job, the last time she made me a carrot cake. For now, I have to leave, I need to go for a walk.

CHAMPAGNE

In my footsteps today

I rarely think of my feet when I walk, but today I do.

With each of my steps, my shoes sink a bit to leave an imprint. It will soon disappear, but for a moment I leave a trace of my passage, a proof of my presence. This ephemeral trail does not disclose my destination, only points to its direction. It is not important as the destination matters not today. I just needed to be here, in my element, where I feel free and peaceful. At the edge of two worlds, where they meet. Today this meeting is dramatic. One world crashes on the other with a loud noise, leaving a trail of foam which I enjoy stepping in. The salt will no doubt ruin my shoes, but salt is one link between my emotions and this world that is not mine, yet that I love so much that I immerse myself in it every chance I get. We are water and both temperamental. A stress, a pressure from beyond can distress us. Our turmoil grows and grows. What started as a ripple of emotions, swells into contagious mountains that affect all around us and can reach far away. The stress turns into energy that can power entire towns, but most times is lost. Sometimes it quietly dissipates. Today the distant power is undeniable and will crash in a beautiful release when it becomes too much for the depth that carries it. It will take repeated effort to die out, and it will break and break and break again at clockwork intervals.

Tomorrow it will all be over. What gets eroded in today's fury, might take months to return. For all that is lost, what will remain will have smoother angles. I will come back here and bathe in the returned quietness. For now, I will walk to my goal and when I get there, turn around and retrace my steps until I get home, invigorated.

A blanket of clouds

My muscles are heavy, and I drop the weight they accumulated today. My whole body breathes a sigh of relief. My pillow is like a feathery cloud under my neck. My duvet hugs me with a soft and heavy warmth. This moment is a deliverance, and my entire body and mind can rest in the serenity of the fading day. I enjoy the silence of the motionless moment. The darkness of my eyelids blends with the darkness of the night. My consciousness dives into depths that negate it.

And soon I am in a different world, one my words fail to describe because when I am there, I access the part of my mind that doesn't know the rational world, the physical and verbal realm. A cerebral place made of my deepest personality, my unaccepted yearnings, my strongest beliefs and unacknowledged fears, my ignored demons, and simplest qualities. And when I regain control of my voice, my body, my thoughts, and my words, I leave this immaterial space. I know this domain exists because it is the gateway where my thoughts take life and where they die. This world is real, and within me, untouched by societal and familial rules and conditioning. It is my core, where the child I once was still lives. Here everything is possible, the best and the worse. Untethered aspirations, guilty aches, and shameful desires, nothing is out of scope. I am true, I am vulnerable, I am naive, I lose myself to find myself, I have no control, this makes me limitless. I can fly, even under water, and swim up hill. I bring back dead people and travel to *familiar* places I have never been to.

If I wake up now, I will take these memories with me. If I drift off and my eyes stop their rapid movement, the memory of these magical moments will be gone, maybe until I return to them another night.

And I do leave this whimsical place. I come back to my bed of clouds; the weightlessness of the dream world crashes back with the gravity of my awakened state. The weight of my duvet, my legs feel heavy, I can't move. The inertia of my mind makes up for the stillness of my body, and my thoughts are rolling free. The irrational gives way to actual preoccupations. But what comes is not the softness of my bed, the memory of the lovely evening, or the tasty meal I had, not the anticipation of the holidays I am planning. No, it is always a jumble of aimless thoughts, and wandering worries. The darkest of my ideas, the illogical fear, the repressed feelings. My dreams have gone through a reality filter to become the 3 AM realistic ruminating, full of inaccuracies, flaws, and exaggerations. The more I push them away, the more vivid they are. If I could sleep, they would go. But to fall asleep, I have to let them go. How many sheep do I have to count? Is that the number for the Sandman?

My night thoughts have the vividity of the day but the muddiness of the night. The rational of my mind and the irrational of my heart. Fatigue has erased the sense of my reasoning and wiped out the safety of my hopes. I want to go back to my dreams; their fantasies are easy to grasp, and they hide the truth of my thoughts.

At last, a yawn. Tired of my own thoughts, I am finally sinking back to the arms of Morpheus. It always seems to happen 5 minutes before the alarm goes off, though.

I am returning to slumber world. Please let it not be where I am naked in a crowd, or worse, at dinner with BoJo. That gorgeous beach I sometimes go to would be a great destination and maybe I could even meet with my long-lost friend. I would love to fly away above the clouds, but to fly in dreams my mind needs to be light and free and not anchored by daytime worries. Wherever I go just before the alarm goes off, I often bring back with me to the early morning and lose it through the day.

Whatever I did not get to in the night, I have a chance to try again during the day.

Our own boat

We are all drifting in water, looking for a boat to rest on. In this tumultuous ocean we are in, some seem to surf the waves effortlessly. For others, the ups and downs are underwater mountains to climb with highs barely breaking the surface and only seeming high because the lows are so deep.

We are rarely alone, but it often feels lonely. Everyone for themselves in the rage of the sea. Some people will try to climb on you to stay afloat or drag you down as they sink. We can try to hold on to each other. Occasionally, someone might just be there beside you, sharing the moment with you. We want to help others, but we need to reach the boat ourselves before we can throw life rings.

In this sea there are no cargo ships, only driftwood, surfboards, canoes, and small dinghies. Hopefully, you will find yours, find your way. Maybe you will find one with someone who will extend a helping hand to pull you on. On rare occasions, you may get a push up from the water and you will want to be the helping hand to pull them on. When you find your craft, I wish you fair winds and following seas.

Until then, keep your head above water, keep breathing, keep swimming. The more you swim, the larger your search circle for this dinghy of yours.

Feeding the fish

There is a puppy in the kitchen. This adorable puppy is the type of dog that barely barks. He wags his tail and greets me with a wobble that I recognize as asking for a nice belly rub. I happily comply and soon realise who this puppy is. I was in charge of this puppy. I was supposed to feed this puppy. Certainly, he must have gone to the neighbour and begged for food. The neighbour would have fed him for sure. Clearly, he found food and water somewhere, enough to survive. He seems excited to see me. How long has it been, though? Well, the important thing is that he is healthy.

There is a bird in a cage, a lovely green budgie. The cage is open, and he flies straight to my shoulder. He is skinny, has lost some feathers it seems. I know because I know this bird. It used to be mine. I thought he was dead. Anyhow, I am glad to see him, but if he were alive all these years, where was he? And also, where was I, who took care of him? His cage is filthy, the water dispenser is empty, the food tray is covered with seed shells and bird droppings. Oh, little bird, I am sorry I have neglected you for so long. I will feed you now and clean this cage. I am here now.

There is a fish in a bowl. I don't know this fish, but somehow, I feel it was my responsibility to feed it. It looks okay. At least it is alive, which for a fish is really all you expect. I don't know how long I had been responsible for this fish. I don't think I ever even fed it. I never even thought of this fish or cared about fish. How did it survive? Clearly the fish did not beg for food from the neighbour. I have the feeling this fish is not real. It is a figment of my imagination. A projection of my busy mind. A light is shone on my doubts, my guilt, my shortcomings.

This fish, this bird, this puppy, they are in me. They are the vulnerable, the free, the playful part of me that I have neglected and forgotten. I am glad they managed to stay alive all this time and have now found their way back to me in my dreams.

Every morning, when I make my breakfast and pack my daughter's lunch, I need to remember to feed the fish, change the water in the cage, and play with the puppy.

A bag of rice

I remember sitting up in a tree with Alex one summer, when we were 12 years old. The leaves were hiding us, but we could see through them. In this tree we watched other kids play and look for us. We had avoided the adults calling us to go home. We watched people arrive and people leave. We once even witnessed a car crash. We had a unique viewpoint over the road, yet the adults dismissed our report of the events. On this summer day, we were in the first row for a conversation that was not intended for us. Alex's father and my mother were discussing the fate of our grandfather's property. The very same property where our tree was. In the shade of this tree, they argued what should be done with the place now that our grandfather was no longer with us. It had been 5 years and apparently was costing an arm and a leg to maintain. At the time I thought it meant the cleaning and gardening were too much for one's set of arms and legs. I promised myself to help more often. My mum wanted to sell the place. Alex's father was looking for ways to offset the cost. We listened silently, trying to make sense of the conversation, and looked at each other with confusion and sadness in our eyes. On both sides some arguments made sense, but equally, some excuses seemed unfair. I was mad at my mother and Alex was proud of his father.

My mother was slowly winning over Alex's father. Family history and sentimental values weighed little against practicality and the reality of the wallet. I wanted to argue that if it needed to be sold because we didn't come often enough, we would visit even less if it were sold. But I did not open my mouth and silently made my case only to myself.

It turned out that summer would be the last time we would climb that tree. When the decision was made to sell, the tree got cut because, as the adults would say, the tree blocked the view from the house and devalued the property.

Again, my thoughts, that by cutting the tree we would reduce the chance that a tree lover would purchase the property, remained private. Up to now, I still regret not saying anything. The tree was cut and burnt and not only ceased to be a carbon sink, but released a fair amount of carbon dioxide when it was pointlessly sent to smoke. But few people cared about these considerations at the time. And I was not educated enough on the matter back then to be able to substantiate my argument.

After the house got sold, we then had to visit each other's family home to be together and somehow our parents rarely found the time or motivation. We grew apart and absence became a habit. As we filled the void with new people and exciting experiences, the sadness of the loss shrunk until one day we almost forgot how much we enjoyed being together. Alex became a distant memory of a closeness from another time when our priorities were different and our lives simpler. The adults' coldness had involuntarily spread to us. Friendship is a fragile plant: it needs caring and feeding. Anything short of that is neglect. We were not on bad terms; we had just become strangers, disconnected enough to not feel the need to hear from each other. I moved away for a while and the distance between us became even more justifiable. Our bond had been put in a dormant state from which I hoped it would one day emerge. Friendship can take many forms. Like a bag of rice tossed in a basket with other groceries when you don't pay attention, it will adopt undefined shapes to find its place. When you bring it home and place it in the pantry, you can lay it to rest on a shelf or stand it up, or shape it into the box you want to put it in. And sometimes, it gets buried behind pasta, flour, or tins… until you are fed up with pasta and look for something else to cook.

We could have continued on this predictable asymptotic trajectory, but one day I received a letter. In it, a photo of the small measly tree. When I looked carefully, I recognized the garden. A tree had been planted where our old tree had once stood. It is an oak tree. One day it will be majestic. From now on, I will make the effort every so often to go check how much it has grown.

The shape of what will be

I feel empty, blank, drained, lost, bare, weightless, free-floating. I struggle to find the precise words to describe how I feel. How do you describe a lack of something? How do you describe an absence, a hole?

Missing something without knowing what you miss. I can only relate to what I know, what I have, or what I have lost. How do I explain wanting something I don't know, yearning for something never met? I know I need it, without even knowing what it is. I'm missing something that may not even exist yet. Before I can search what I am longing for, don't I need to know what it is? This might help define where and how to look for it.

I won't claim to understand Welsh, but there is a Welsh word which is close to expressing how I feel today. Hiraeth – it describes a type of homesickness, but for a home to which you can't return or that never existed.

Maybe finding shouldn't be the objective. Maybe the search, the process of preparing myself for what is to come will asymptotically bring me towards what I miss.

Not everything has a meaningful goal, a desirable destination. Take life, for example. Its destination is death. What matters is the path between birth and death, not the extremities. Every moment in between is life. It is made up of memorable days but also of empty hours, the ones you sat in a dentist waiting room, the hours you slept, the hours you tried to escape reality.

If I had the choice, I would spend my time on a beach. Swimming in the water, playing with the sand.

When you press something in compacted sand, you create a mould of it. The shape that remains can be used to replicate the part that was moulded. Now imagine something you want. Mentally press it in the sand and imagine its shape. How much sand did you need, a bucketful, a swimming pool, an entire beach? How do you know how much sand you need for what is possible but unknown? The full potential of your mould will only be limited by how much sand you have available. Life does not make moulds out of sand; it casts its shape in us. People and events leave marks on us. We miss the past or embrace the memories, but the future is unknown. We can dream it, we can plan it, but it will surprise us.

I want to open a door, or a gate, to the unknown,

expand from the inside, have the longest beach I can to mould my full potential. Is it a 5- or 7-mile beach? Is Arcachon to Tarnos long enough? Why even put limits? I need to grow, grow my heart, and grow my mind, grow my beach to welcome even the unimaginable. This gaping hole in me is not empty, it is infinite, it is full of possibilities. Trying to fill the void will go against its growth. This hole is my beach, my blank page. Today, I take my first step on this beach. I leave footsteps in the sand, and words on paper, and serve them to my friends.

CHAMPAGNE

CHAMPAGNE

CHAMPAGNE

건배 Một hai ba yo

Proost Kanpai شاباش, بو خوش

Şerefe

наздраве Skål Salut Iechyd Da

干杯 Prost

Gon bui

Manuia Gin cin Santé ΥΓΕΙΑ

Salud Sláinte Mabuhay

Biba Živjeli Cheers Saúde לחיים

На здоровье YEC'HED MAT наздраве Prosit

Mahafaly

Dô Vô Nazdravlje Oldik Kia ora

Impilo

Bottoms up Topa Kāmau

CHAMPAGNE

Printed in Great Britain
by Amazon